The Rejected Princess and Other Stories
Stories from the Mahabharat

Swapna Dutta

Ukiyoto Publishing

All global publishing rights are held by

Ukiyoto Publishing

Published in 2022

Content Copyright © Swapna Dutta

ISBN 9789360160920

All rights reserved.
No part of this publication may be reproduced, transmitted, or stored in a retrieval system, in any form by any means, electronic, mechanical, photocopying, recording or otherwise, without the prior permission of the publisher.

The moral rights of the author have been asserted.

This is a work of fiction. Names, characters, businesses, places, events, locales, and incidents are either the products of the author's imagination or used in a fictitious manner. Any resemblance to actual persons, living or dead, or actual events is purely coincidental.

This book is sold subject to the condition that it shall not by way of trade or otherwise, be lent, resold, hired out or otherwise circulated, without the publisher's prior consent, in any form of binding or cover other than that in which it is published.

www.ukiyoto.com

Acknowledgements

Expelled from Heaven, The Rejected Princess and Amba's Revenge appeared in Chandamama; A Debt Repaid and The Ultimate Sacrifice appeared in Children's World (Children's Book Trust). The Vow appeared in Children's World and also The School Magazine (NSW, Australia).

Foreword

The Mahabharat, one of the two great epics of India, depicts life on earth and human beings in all their myriad shades. There is a popular saying that what does not find a place in the Mahabharat, be it good or bad, simply does not exist. It is the story of human beings with all their goodness and virtues as well as faults, frailties and weaknesses.

In the age of the Mahabharat people lived life king-size. A son thought nothing of renouncing the throne and with it, his life's happiness, for the sake of seeing his father happy. A celestial river could readily agree to go down on earth, marry a human being and give birth to eight young brothers at their pleading. A princess, unfairly rejected by her lover, could pray so hard, so earnestly and for so long that Lord Shiva himself could be moved and grant her the boon of destroying the man who had ruined her life. A sage who was otherwise perfect could possess such a massive ego about not keeping his promise that he could readily demand an obnoxious and cruel sacrifice from an innocent and devoted disciple. In the Mahabharat one sees a man at his best and and at his worst and how good and evil always manage to co-exist side by side.

There are millions of stories in the Mahabharat quite apart from the main story. Nearly all of them have been retold by many writers in many different languages. And yet no two re-telling is the same because the great epic means something different to each writer who sees it in his/her own light. The basic facts may be the same but the focus of the stories and the interpretation are not quite the same. Each re-teller has his/her own point of view which makes it distinct and different.

Contents

Expelled from Heaven	1
The Vow	9
The Rejected Princess	15
Amba's Revenge	20
A Debt Repaid	24
The Ultimate Sacrifice	35
About the Author	*39*

Expelled from Heaven

The Vasu brothers were visiting the hermitage of sage Vashistha. Eight brothers, popularly known as the *AstaVasu*, were inmates of heaven. But they often came down to earth to visit the great sages. They particularly admired sage Vashishta and this visit was a special one. The brothers had brought along the youngest bride to receive his blessings because the sage could not be present at the wedding. But on reaching his hermitage they found that he was away. His young disciples told them that he was expected to return shortly so they should wait for him. If they cared to, they could see the garden in the mean time.

The Vasu brothers and the young bride looked around them eagerly. One of the young hermits volunteered to show them around. After taking a look at the lush green fields, where flowers bloomed in a riot of colours, and the fruit orchards they walked over to the cowshed where Nandini, the celestial cow, stood placidly. She was a special favourite with everyone in the hermitage. The young hermit told the bride about Nandini's special powers. Not only did her milk taste like nectar but anyone who drank it lived for ten thousand years without any illness. What's more, she had an unlimited supply of milk.

"Is that really true?" asked the bride incredulously.

"Of course it is," said the hermit as he shut the door of the cowshed. "Our Nandini is really wonderful. I thought everyone knew about her!"

"Know about whom? Who are you talking about?" asked Deu, the youngest of the Vasu brothers, looking first at his bride and then at the young hermit.

"Nandini," she cried excitedly pointing to the snow-white cow, "Is she really as wonderful as this hermit brother says?"

"Yes, indeed she is," said Deu with a smile, "In fact sage Vashishta himself has miraculous powers. There isn't a thing that he can't do. When you see him you'll realise what I'm talking about." Sudarshana, the young bride, shrugged and looked the other way. "All sages have special powers. There's nothing wonderful about that. It's Nandini I'm thinking of. What a wonderful creature to possess!"

"True," agreed her husband.

The young hermit had many other duties. So he left the young couple in the garden and went to attend to them.

"I wonder what the old sage does with so much milk," she said pensively, "Surely he can't be drinking it all?"

"Good heavens! No! What a mad idea!" said Deu laughing.

"I can't think why a sage should hold on to a cow like her when he doesn't need her in the least," she said petulantly. "She'd be of great use to people like us."

"You can ask him for Nandini when you meet the sage," said her husband lightly. "He is a great one for giving away things."

"What! Beg for a cow!" cried Sudarshana raising her eyebrows, "You forget that I am a king's daughter! I have never had to beg for anything yet!"

But what she presently suggested was far more outrageous than begging. As the sage was away and not likely to return for some time she suggested that they should all go back home. "And let's take the cow with us," she added.

"Take Nandini?" cried Deu horrified, "you must be off your head! Surely, you're not thinking of stealing her?"

"I would hardly call it 'stealing,'" said Sudarshana, blushing in spite of herself, "It would be making good use of her. She is just being wasted here."

"Well, I'm not going in for theft, and neither are you! Not if I know it!" said Deu firmly.

Sudarshana tried to get around her husband by coaxing.

"Aren't you making a mountain of a molehill?" she said in her most persuasive tone. "You say that he's always giving away things. Well, then, he'll merely think that someone who needs a cow has taken her!"

"We ought to ask him first," said Deu, frowning.

"Of course, we'd have asked him if he had been here," said Sudarshana, smiling her sweetest, "but as he isn't here, how can we? I'm sure he won't mind! No if he is really as great as you say he is."

"But," said Deu hesitantly, "but...."

"There are no 'buts' about it," said Sudarshana with gleaming eyes. "Go and tell your brothers while I fetch her from the shed. Luckily there isn't a soul around."

Though the other seven Vasu brothers were amazed at the idea of taking away Nandini, Deu managed to convince them that it was all right, if slightly unusual. As no one at the hermitage suspected them of doing anything irregular no one bothered to keep a watch on their activities. It was quite easy for the brothers to walk out of the hermitage with Nandini while everyone else was busy inside.

Sage Vashishta returned home after a while. He saw immediately that Nandini was missing. He just had to concentrate for a second to learn what had happened. He instantly knew that the Vasu brothers had stolen her. He felt astonished as well as very angry. It was not just because they had taken away Nandini. He could not understand or forgive any inmate of heaven indulging in theft!

He summoned the Vasu brothers without losing any time."You are not worthy of heaven!" he told them contemptuously, "So I expel you from your heavenly abode! Go down to the earth! Be born as human beings. Experience human joy and sorrow for an entire lifetime. Then and then alone will you realize what you have lost. And realize the gravity of your sin!"

"But, my Lord," said the eldest of the Vasu brothers, "Please allow me tell you what actually happened."

"I know what you are going to say," said Vashishta interrupting him, "you are going to tell me that it was not your own idea but that of your sister-in-law."

"Yes," said the brothers in a chorus.

"Unfortunately that does not take away your responsibility or lessen your sin in any way," said Vasistha, "All of you are older than she is. You need not have listened to her, nor allowed her to influence you. You should have made her see that stealing is a sin."

"But…" faltered Deu ….

The sage gave him a scathing look. "As her husband, you ought to have stopped her. But you joined forces with her instead and dragged your brothers into it! Shame on you!"

The brothers fell at his feet and begged for mercy. But the sage stood firm. He looked at the brothers and said, "Deu is the actual culprit and drew the rest of you in. Your fault lay in listening to him. So seven of you will be born on earth but will soon return to heaven. But Deu must pay for his sin by spending his entire life on earth."

The Vasu brothers were devastated and heartbroken. For inmates of heaven, to be condemned to a lifetime on earth was the greatest imaginable punishment.

"We cannot be born as the children of a commoner," said Deu, looking more upset than the others. "We must at least have a noble father and mother. What shall we do?"

"I am almost sure that sage Vasistha will let us choose our parents," said one of his elder brothers, "He is basically very kind."

"I feel the same," said the next brother, "We can't really blame him for punishing us. We deserve it after doing such a terrible thing."

"Who we should choose for our father?" asked Deu.

"What about Prateep, the king of Hastinapur?" suggested the eldest brother.

"He is too old," said Deu shaking his head, "What's more, he is about to retire and take up a life of meditation in the forest."

"What about his son, Prince Shantanu? He is a splendid young man - kind, brave and just," said another.

"Right! He could be our father," said the brothers together.

"And it would be wonderful to have the Ganga, the celestial river, for our mother, if only we can persuade her to go down on earth as a human being," said Deu.'

"Yes," agreed the others, "She is so sacred and pure. We wouldn't mind being born as human beings if we were her sons." "Come on, then. Let's all go to her without wasting any more time," said Deu, "I'm sure she will come to our rescue if we plead hard enough."

The brothers went to Ganga and prostrated before her.

"Mother, we've come to ask a favour of you and we just won't take 'no' for an answer," they said in a chorus.

"Very well," said Ganga smiling at them, "What is it?"

"Remember that it's a promise," said Deu. "You can't go back on your word once you have given it!"

"What on earth is it?" asked Ganga intrigued. "Why all this mystery?"

We beg of you to go down to the earth as a woman and marry prince Shantanu. We eight brothers want to be reborn as your sons."

"Surely you can't be serious?" said Ganga looking at their downcast faces, "What on earth have you been doing? Why do you want such a strange promise?"

They told her about what they had done and the curse of sage Vashishta. Ganga listened attentively and realized the depth of their despair. She agreed to help them out. But they would have to wait for what Ganga considered to be the right time. The Vasu brothers had to agree to her terms and went back with a heavy heart, hating the thought of being punished.

Old king Pratip had just crowned his son Shantanu as the ruler of Hastinapur and went to the forest to embrace a life of prayers and meditations. Shantanu turned out to be an excellent ruler, loved and respected by his people. One day, as he was walking alone by the riverside, Ganga appeared before him in the guise of a beautiful girl.

Shantanu was charmed by her loveliness. He had never come across such ethereal beauty before! She looked just like a goddess!

"I neither know nor care WHO you are!" cried Shantanu impulsively, "I love you and must have you for my queen. Will you marry me? I shall strive to make you happy with all I have!"

"Yes I will," said Ganga with a charming smile, "But on one condition."

"What is it?" asked Shantanu recklessly, "I agree to your condition, whatever it is."

"You must promise me that you shall never criticize me or forbid me to do anything I may choose to do, whether you approve of my action or not," said Ganga. "Is that all?" said Shantanu looking relieved. "I wouldn't ever dream of forbidding you to do anything !"

"You must allow me to do whatever I want to. The slightest protest from you, and I shall leave you immediately and forever. Do you agree?" asked Ganga, flashing another charming smile. "I agree, my Queen," said Shantanu, dizzy with happiness, "I promise to let you have your own way in everything without protest. On my honour as a king!"

So Shantanu and Ganga were married. They loved each other deeply and were as happy as two mortals could possibly be. When a son was born to them, the entire kingdom rejoiced. One day, the queen went out with the baby and came back alone." "Where's the little prince?" asked Shantanu surprised.

"I threw him into the river Ganges," said Ganga casually.

Shantanu was stunned. Had the queen gone raving mad? Whoever heard of a mother throwing away her own child into the river? He was about to remonstrate against her cruel act, but checked himself, remembering his promise. He had already lost his son; he could not bear the thought of losing his queen as well.

When another son was born to them, the queen did the same thing and threw him into the river. The king suffered in silence. Hadn't he promised, on his honour, not to question any action of the queen? How could he possibly break his word? He merely prayed that the queen might be cured of her madness. She was so sweet and loving in other ways. Why did she behave like this whenever she became a mother? Shantanu wondered but could find no answer.

Seven sons were born to them in all and the queen threw each and every one of them into the river. Shantanu was heartbroken and could bear no more. So, when the eighth son was born, he would not let the child out of his sight for a moment. One night he dozed off while sitting by the cradle. He suddenly woke up to see the queen lifting the baby quietly and walking away with stealthy steps. He followed her. Ganga did not turn back. Obviously she was not aware that she was being followed.

They reached the bank of the river in total darkness. But as soon as Ganga tried to throw the baby into the water, Shantanu caught hold of her hand. "Don't!" he cried out in agony, "Please don't do it! How can you be so cruel and so heartless, Ganga? Aren't you the mother of this innocent child? You've already killed seven of our sons. Let this one live, for God's sake!"

"Very well," said Ganga placing the sleeping child in his arms, "He is yours and you can bring him up. But I can't live with you any more!"

"Not live with me?" asked Shantanu bewildered.

"Have you forgotten your promise?" asked the queen. "Didn't I tell you that I would leave you the moment you questioned anything I chose to do?"

"I stopped you for the sake of my son!" cried Shantanu. "Haven't you had your own way in every single thing all these years? Have I ever uttered a word in protest? Or make the least attempt to stop you? You cannot leave me just because I begged for the life of our child. It wouldn't be fair! I don't believe you can be so heartless."

"But I am afraid I must leave you now, Shantanu. You see, I have no reason to stay here any longer !" said Ganga softly, "I am sorry, but that's how it is." The sincerity and intensity of Shantanu's grief pained her. But she had to tell him the truth now.

"Listen to me," she said, sitting beside him, "You don't know who I really am or why I married you."

Shantanu said nothing but continued to look at her with grief-stricken eyes while Ganga told him the story of the Vasu brothers, their theft of Nandini and their expulsion from heaven. She told him of her promise to help them – the sole fact that had made her come down to the earth in the guise of a woman and marry him.

"The years with you have been wonderfully happy ones," she added wistfully,"but you must realize that I can't remain here any longer. My true place is in heaven."

Shantanu nodded sorrowfully, unable to speak.

"Look after our son, Devabrata," said Ganga. "I know he'll be a good son to you and you will be proud of him some day."

"Yes," said Shantanu, holding him tight.

"Don't grieve for me, dear Shantanu," said Ganga, "You shall find happiness once again, I promise you. "

"Shall I?" asked Shantanu in a voice devoid of feeling, "Happiness no longer seems either important or possible."

"Be brave and think of our son," said Ganga, "Remember, I leave him in your care."

Then she disappeared into the clouds. Shantanu stood still, baby Devabrata in his arms. Little did he imagine how brave and great the child would become in the years to come.

The Vow

"I tell you, Father, it's the most wonderful horse I've ever seen!" The eyes of the young prince shone with eagerness as he leaned on his father's arms.

"Is it?" King Shantanu had a far away look in his eyes and did not sound particularly interested.

"It runs so fast, just like the lightning! It really does," continued the prince in the same eager tone, "Do come with me and see it, father"

"I'm glad you are pleased", said King Shantanu in a languid voice. But he did not get up.

"It would be so marvelous to ride it in the battlefield," said the prince, disappointed by his father's lukewarm response, "Don't you want to see it?"

"See it? No, not now" said the king listlessly, "I don't feel up to it, Devabrata. Don't tease me."

At once the prince was all concern. "You're not ill, are you, Father?" he cried in an anxious voice, "Should I send for the royal physician?"

"I'm not ill, son," said the king in a reassuring voice. "But I feel tired. I want to be alone. You go and ride that horse. I'm sure it is as good as you say."

Prince Devabrata turned away. But his eyes betrayed his anxiety. King Shantanu had been behaving so strangely of late! He was always preoccupied and did not seem interested in anything. And yet . . . he had not reached the age when one loses interest in worldly things! He was still at the peak of his power. Although prince Devabrata had been crowned the prince-regents some days back he was still little more than a boy.

Young Devabrata was the light of his father's eyes and was adored by the entire kingdom. He was the son of Shantanu's first queen Ganga who had come down from heaven to marry him. She had now returned to heaven, leaving the little child with his father. Shantanu had brought him up alone. Devabrata was now an accomplished young man. He had mastered each and every art necessary for a king and was already a great warrior. Parasurama, the renowned warrior, had himself taught Devabrata and had declared that there was nothing more which he could teach the young prince. "He would make a great king, some day!" Parasurama had predicted proudly.

King Shantanu was very happy with his son. In fact, he felt relieved at the thought that if ever he grew too tired or frail to carry on his duties as king, Devabrata would be able to take over from him and be a greater king than he had been. That was why he had insisted on crowing him as the prince regent despite his being so young. It had seemed the right thing to do.

As Devabrata walked towards the royal stables he recalled the earlier times when he and his father had been such good companions. They had shared all kinds of adventures like two comrades! King Shantanu had marvelled at his son's ability to grasp things. He seemed to be a born ruler and leader of people. How enthusiastically had he made plans for his son! How happy and eager had he been and how very proud every time Devabrata had learned something new! Where had all the old enthusiasm gone, Devabrata wondered sadly. His father still loved him as much as ever but his heart as well as mind seemed to be elsewhere. He's unhappy about something, thought Devabrata. But what could it possibly be? Surely everything was within a king's reach? He silently resolved to get to the bottom of the matter.

Just then he looked up and saw someone riding towards the stables. It was one of the king's ministers. Devabrata's face lit up as the rider alighted from his horse and saluted him.

"I'm happy to see you, Sir," said Devabrata smiling at him. "I was just about to go and look you up myself."

"Why? Was there a particular reason?"

"I'm worried about father," said Devabrata simply.

"Worried about his majesty?" asked the minister looking surprised, "But why? He is perfectly well as far as we know."

"I'm not worried about his health," said Devabrata shaking his head, "I'm afraid he is not happy and perhaps worried about something." The minister stared at him. "What makes you think that? Has he said anything?" he asked.

"No. But he isn't like himself. He is listless and absent-minded and doesn't seem interested in anything," said Devabrata, "And he hardly ever speaks to me these days. It isn't like him!"

"And you've never asked him what is wrong?" asked the minister, looking keenly at Devabrata.

"He says there is nothing wrong," said Devabrata looking troubled. "I sometime wonder if . . . . ." he stopped short suddenly.

"Yes?" said the minister gently.

"I wonder if he feels lonely," said Devabrata. "I am no longer a child needing his full attention and I'm very busy most of the time . . ."

"It would be strange if he weren't lonely," said the minister, "Your mother left him a long time ago. We have all asked him to remarry several times but he has always brushed aside the idea."

"I wish I could see him happy again!" said Devabrata eagerly. "I would do anything and give anything for his happiness. My father has always been everything to me!"

"I'll look into this," promised the minister, "And if there is anything you can do, I shall tell you about it. Cheer up! You don't want *him* to start worrying about *you*, do you?"

Devabrata thanked him and went off for a ride. When king Shantanu saw him ride past his balcony, his heart warmed with pride. "I cannot do it," he said wistfully to himself. "I cannot possibly cheat Devabrata of his inheritance for the sake of my own happiness. It would be wrong and a grave injustice!" The king leaned across the window gazing towards the river.

Devabrata was right. King Shantanu was really unhappy and it seemed that he could never be happy again. He was in love once again but that love demanded a price that he could not pay. The king picked up a lotus from the gold vase, smelt it, sighed, and laid it aside. It was the same fragrance that had waylaid him some days earlier in the depth of the forest. He had followed the fragrance and found himself beside a river. There he saw a beautiful girl who took people across in a rowboat. She was Satyavati, the daughter of a fisherman. It was she who smelt like a lotus.

Such beauty in a fisherman's hut? The king was incredulous at first. But he lost his heart instantly and decided that if any girl could fill the void left by Ganga and make him happy once again, it was this lotus maiden. He had found the fisherman and asked for his daughter's hand. Who, after all, could refuse King Shantanu? Certainly not one of his own subjects! But the unexpected had happened. The fisherman though highly gratified, refused to give Satyavati in marriage unless King Shantanu gave his word of honour that the son born to Satyavati would be the next king!

"But that is not possible!" said the king at once, "I have a son already. No one but Devabrata can be the king after me."

"Then you can't have my daughter," said the fisherman firmly, "She is not going to be just a part of the royal crowd. If she cannot be the mother of the future king, she shall not wed you at all!"

King Shantanu had pleaded, begged and implored the fisherman to think again. How could the king do such grave injustice to the crown prince? And what would the people say? They loved their prince just as much as he did! King Shantanu was too honourable to take Satyavati away by force which he might have done. He returned home with a broken heart instead.

Devabrata went to see the minister again after a few days.

"Well, sir," he asked impatiently, "Have you been able to find out anything?"

"Yes," said the minister looking straight into Devabrata's eyes, "Your father is in love with Satyavati, a fisherman's daughter. But she refuses to wed him."

"Refuses to wed him?" cried Devabrata incredulously, "Refuses to wed the King of the land? Is she mad? Where does she live? I shall go to her myself and make her agree! Imagine refusing someone like my father!"

The minister told the prince where Satyavati lived. He rode at once to the fisherman's cottage. Sayavati's father saluted him gravely.

"I am Devabrata," the prince told him without any preamble. "Your daughter is going to be our new queen and my new mother. I have come to fetch her. Where is she?"

"It is kind of you, Sir, but I have already told his majesty that he shall not wed her unless she is given her rightful position."

"Her rightful position? What on earth can you mean? I don't understand you."

"I shall tell you frankly what I mean," said the fisherman, "My daughter shall not marry the king unless he promises that the son born to her shall be the next king"

"Is that all?" said Devabrata looking relieved. "Well, there is no need to bring my father into this. I promise you, here and now, that the son born to your daughter shall be the king. I shall never claim my father's throne. I am not merely the crown prince but a *kshatriya* (the warrior class) as well. I will not break my word even if I die."

"Do you mean it?" cried the fisherman in a disbelieving voice, "You'd give up the throne – your rightful heritage – just like that?"

"Yes, I would, for the sake of my father," said Devabrata in a voice that left no room for doubt.

"Well, you may keep your word," said the fisherman, "I'm not doubting that. But, what about your sons? They might fight for the throne, you know!"

"They will not," said Devabrata, "There will not be any sons. I shall never marry nor take a woman as my companion. Now, are you satisfied?"

"Not marry all you life?" cried the fisherman again.

"All my life," said Devabrata firmly.

"Do you know what you are promising?" asked the fisherman in a choked voice, "Have you considered all that it implies?"

For a second, colourful visions flooded the mind of the young prince. Visions of ruling the kingdom he loved so much. Visions of power, conquest and glory. Visions of love and companionship. Visions of young children, as brave as him. But only for a second.

"You would renounce life in all its glory and live the life of an ascetic? Just for your father's sake?" asked the fisherman.

"I would gladly lay down my life for my father," said Devabrata, "Giving up the throne isn't very much."

Instantly, the whole place lit up as if by magic. Angels who had heard Devabrata's promise showered flowers on him from above. And they leaned out to catch a glimpse of his face. "It is a great promise! A brave and difficult promise!" said the angels above,"Devabrata, you shall henceforth be known as *Bheeshma* (one who makes a tough promise) because of this vow."

The news soon reached King Shantanu at his palace and he came out to see for himself if it was true. He embraced Devabrata. "I bless you my son, bless you for your great sacrifice. I grant you the boon that you shall die only when you want to. You shall decide when to leave this world."

Devabrata bowed down and touched his father's feet.

The Rejected Princess

"I do feel excited about tomorrow," said Ambika looking out of the window.

"The hall looks gorgeous – all decorated and lit up," remarked Ambalika, "But I feel more scared than excited."

"Scared?" asked Amba looking up from the garland of flowers she was weaving, "What is there to be scared about? All *Kshatriya* princesses have to face the *swayamvara*, the special ceremony where they select their own husbands. It's a simple custom, as old as the hills."

"It may be simple for *you*," said Ambika giving her a meaningful look, "But it isn't at all simple for either Ambalika or myself!"

"You're right," agreed Ambalika with a nervous laugh, "I just can't imagine which prince I'm going to choose. There are too many of them!"

"You are lucky to know your own mind," she said to Amba.

"Yes", added Ambika with a wink, "You will make a beeline for a certain person while poor Ambalika and I will be fumbling around with our garlands, not knowing where to place them!"

Amba, the eldest of the three sisters, blushed but did not reply. The other two continued to tease her. They knew that Amba had already given her heart to young King Shalva who often visited the king of Varanasi, their father. He was sure to be present at the *swayamvara* the next day. Ambika and Ambalika were too young to know their own minds and had formed no attachments. But they knew that kings and princes from all over the land would be present, eager to win the three princesses of Varanasi. Everyone knew about their beauty and accomplishments. Any king would consider himself lucky to be selected by one of them.

"Are you thinking of garlanding the king of Karnataka, Ambika?" asked Aambalika with a naughty grin.

"Not me!" said Ambika promptly, "He is much too fat."

"The king of Ujjain, then?"

"He is said to have a bare patch right above his forehead. I'm not going to choose a bald husband!"

"What about the prince of Bidarbha?"

"He is as thin as a fishing rod," said Ambika turning up her dainty nose. "I only hope there will be a few young and good looking princes among our suitors."

"Both of you are being very silly," said Amba from her corner, "There will be many kings and princes, both brave and handsome, and you know it."

"Well, the prince of Hastinapur is said to be both," said Ambika.

"Prince Bheeshma? He won't be present at the *swayamvara* tomorrow," remarked Amba.

"Why ever not?" asked Ambika and Ambalika together.

"He has taken a vow not to marry and not ascend his father's throne despite being the eldest prince."

"Indeed?" said the sisters, "What a strange thing to do!"

"Bheeshma has a young brother, though. I suppose he'll be there."

"It will be awful to be parted from you both," said Ambika, "We have always been together."

"Should we choose neighbouring princes then?" asked Ambalika, "Perhaps that would solve our problem".

But fate had other plans for them. As the sisters sat laughing and joking in Varanasi, Prince Bheeshma at Hastinapur sat looking out of the window pensively. Vichitrabeerya, his young step-brother, was out in the woods. Bheeshma stood up as queen Satyavati, his widowed stepmother, came into the room. It was because of her that he had taken the vow of celibacy and had renounced his right to the throne. His father had been in love with Satyavati and she had vowed not to marry him unless he promised to give the throne to the eldest son born to her. Bheeshma had sacrificed his inheritance to make his father happy. He had devoted all his time to looking after his stepbrothers after the old king died so that they might be fit to manage their own kingdom when old enough.

"Bheeshma," said Satyavati without any preamble, "Have you heard about the *swayamvara* being hosted by the king of Varanasi? I want Vichitrabeerya to be present there."

"I had been thinking the same thing," said Bheeshma. "In fact, I have planned it all out carefully. Just leave it to me."

The day of the *swayamvara* arrived. The royal courtyard of Varanasi was packed to capacity. There were princes and kings galore, all looking their best. The spectators formed a solid wall on all sides, talking excitedly amongst themselves. Suddenly there was a hush.

"Here they come!" whispered the people eagerly.

Amba, Ambika and Ambalika were indeed visions of beauty. People held their breath as they looked at the sisters carrying magnificent garlands made of fragrant flowers. Several hearts missed a beat. Whom would they choose? King Shalva had a confident smile on his lips. He had no doubt about his future. His eyes lit up as they met Amba's in triumphant acknowledgement. But before she could garland him Amba found her hand held in a firm clasp. She was too dazed to cry out as she was forcibly dragged into a chariot along with her two sisters.

"I am Bheeshma of Hastinapura," announced their captor in a loud voice addressing the courtyard full of people, "I am taking away the three princesses to wed them to my brother. Stop me if you can." And the chariot sped away like a gust of wind.

Carrying away a princess by force was an accepted mode of marriage among the *Kshatriyas*. In fact, it was greatly admired because it spelt bravery, romance and adventure. Only the very dashing among the princes tried to do it. Everyone present knew about Bheeshma's vow so it did not appear strange that he should capture the princesses by proxy. The king of Varanasi merely smiled and said, "I'm sure my daughters are going to be very happy. And they will be together." He did not know about Amba and king Shalva's love for each other.

Shalva, however took it as a great insult. So did the other princes. What right had Bheeshma to sneak in and take the princesses away by force? And who was Vichitrabeerya, anyway? A mere child existing safely in his brother's shadow and didn't even have a voice of his own! The assembled kings and princes picked up their weapons and rushed after Bheeshma. But Bheeshma was more than a match for all of them taken together. His arrows showered like rain and his opponents scattered like leaves before a storm. Ambika and Ambalika looked on, interested. Here was bravery indeed! But Amba's eyes flashed with wrath. Tears streamed down her cheeks as she saw Shalva fall from his horse in a crumpled heap. "Brute!" she cried, "Oh you heartless brute! How I hate you for spoiling my life – mine and Shalva's."

The three princesses were welcomed rapturously at Hastinapur. Satyavati came out to welcome them and tell them how happy she was to have them for her daughters-in-law. Ambika and Ambalika liked her on sight. Amba looked away, tears of anger and pain rolling down her cheeks.

"I'm sorry I had to bring you here by force but you are going to be very happy as our queens," said Bheeshma apologetically.

"I cannot be happy here and I cannot accept your brother as my husband," said Amba looking him straight in the eyes.

"Why not?" asked Bheeshma, puzzled.

"Because I love someone else and he loves me too. I would have garlanded him today."

"I am sorry I did not know about it or I would never have brought you here," said Bheeshma in a repentant voice, "Tell me who he is and I shall take you back to him at once. After all, you haven't been married to my brother as yet."

"It is King Shalva." said Amba.

"Come along and get into my chariot," said Bheeshma, "We shall be there in no time."

But when Bheeshma took her there Shalva refused to accept Amba.

"I cannot marry a girl who has been forcibly carried away by another man," he said refusing to look into Amba's tearful eyes.

"But they have all been extremely nice and honourable," protested Amba, "Bheeshma brought me here the moment I told him about you."

"You are no longer fit to be the queen of my kingdom," said Shalva heartlessly. He was still seething with rage.

"But it was not my fault that I was carried away," cried Amba, distraught with grief, "What shall I do? Where shall I go? I shall not return to Varanasi to be pitied by my own people."

"In that case, better see if Bheeshma will have you," said Shalva with a bitter laugh.

It broke Amba's heart to hear Shalva's words.

"I am sorry, Amba," said Bheeshma looking into her tragic eyes, "Any other man of honour would have willingly wed you under the circumstances. But I cannot break my vow even for your sake."

"Sorry!" cried Amba in a bitter voice, "Sorry after you have ruined my life! Is that all you can say?"

"My vow to my father is more important to me than my honour," said Bheeshma.

"How I hate you!" cried Amba, her eyes flashing, "You have messed up my life and ruined all hope of happiness. But do not imagine I shall take it lying down just because I am a woman. I shall have my revenge! I will, I will!" And Amba walked out steadily into the dark, lonely night.

Amba's Revenge

As Amba walked alone under the pale starlight she wondered what she would do. Returning home to her father was unthinkable. She could not possibly have everyone pitying her for the rest of her life! As the eldest of the princesses she had taken the lead in everything and everyone had admired her. She could not imagine the shame of being an object of compassion henceforth. Strangely enough, she did not feel bitter towards Shalva who had refused to accept her. All her anger was directed towards Bheeshma who had carried her from the *swayamvara* by force. It was Bheeshma who had ruined her life making it impossible for Shalva to wed her. He should be made to pay the price. "I shall destroy him," cried Amba a fire raging inside her heart.

But it was not an easy task! And she had no idea how she should go about it. She approached one sage after another and asked for their advice. They merely looked at her in amusement. "Destroy Bheeshma? How can you, child? He is a brave and invincible warrior."

"Besides, he didn't do anything very dreadful," said another, "How was he to know that you loved Shalva? Even your own father knew nothing about it."

They told her to forget the incident, return to Varanasi and marry someone else, someone worthy of her. Surely there were kings enough! One of them suggested sending for Shalva and persuading him to marry her.

"Never!" cried Amba, her eyes flashing. "I shall not force myself on him or anyone else."

"Why don't you go to sage Parasurama?" suggested another, "He taught Bheeshma the art of warfare. He might be able to tell you how to conquer him." The sage was only half serious when he said it but

Amba left for Parasurama's abode instantly. Although it took her several days she sought him out and told him her story.

Parasurama believed in justice and admired people who had the courage to demand it. He was impressed by Amba's determination. His heart went out to the poor unhappy girl whose life seemed to be in shambles. "What would you like to do?" he asked her gently.

"I wish to fight and defeat Bheeshma," cried Amba.

"But you can't, dear. You are a girl. No *Kshatriya* will fight a girl. It's totally against the ethics of warfare."

"Then what am I to do?"

"I shall fight him on your behalf," said Parasurama.

Amba bowed and touched his feet, "Thank you, my Lord," she whispered.

So Parasurama challenged Bheeshma to fight with him. Bheeshma accepted the challenge reluctantly because he hated the thought of fighting his own teacher whom he revered like his own father. A fierce combat raged between the two lasting for several days. Ultimately it was Bheeshma who won. Parasurama told Amba sadly that there was nothing more that he could do.

"Then Lord Shiva remains my only refuge," said Amba in a determined voice, "I shall pray to him and keep on praying until he listens to me."

Amba went into the heart of the forest and sat down to meditate. She prayed earnestly and with all her heart. Days melted into weeks, weeks into months and months into years. And still Amba continued to pray. She prayed looking up at the glaring sun during the torrid months of summer. She stood praying neck deep in icy cold water in the freezing months of winter. Storms raged and gales swept across her body. Rain and hail lashed on her face. But Amba did not waver. Nor did she stop her prayers for a single second. Lord Shiva could bear it no longer and appeared before her. "I am pleased, my child," he told her with a smile, "You shall have your heart's desire. What is it you want from me?"

"I want to fight Bheeshma and defeat him. But I cannot, as a woman. Please find a way."

"You shall be reborn as Shikhandi, the son of king Drupada and you shall fight Bheeshma in the battle of Kurukshetra," pronounced Lord Shiva.

Years flew by. Vichitrabeerya, Bheeshma's step brother, died early. It was Bheeshma again who brought up his two sons – Dhritarashtra and Pandu - and their children, known as the Kauravas and the Pandavas respectively. Although the throne of Hastinapur rightfully belonged to the eldest Pandava prince, the eldest Kaurava prince grabbed it and declared war on the Pandavas, leading to the famous battle of Kurukshetra. Bheeshma's heart yearned for the Pandavas. But loyalty bound him to the kingdom of Hastinapur, held by the Kauravas.

Amba, reborn as prince Shikhandi, was a staunch ally and supporter of the Pandavas. Amba (*we shall continue to refer to her as "Amba" despite being reborn as prince Shikhandi*) remembered who she really was, and why she had been granted the life of a prince. The only other person who knew her secret was Bheeshma. Amba couldn't wait to confront Bheeshma on the battlefield. As a prince she now knew how to fight though she could never be Bheeshma's equal. But she wouldn't mind dying fighting Bheeshma! The very thought of facing him as an equal on the battlefield was worth all the trouble of being reborn as a man!

On the eve of the great battle Yudhisthira, the eldest Pandava prince went to Bheeshma to seek his blessings. "We hate the thought of fighting with you," he said wistfully, "But no *Kshatriya* can refuse a challenge."

"No, of course you can't. But don't be upset. I know you shall win this battle," said Bheeshma.

"But how can we, when you are on the other side?" he asked incredulously, "No one can ever defeat you, Grand-uncle!"

"I'll tell you how you can," said Bheeshma. "I shall not fight Shikhandi. I shall throw my weapons down if she is around."

"*She?* What do you mean? Shikhandi is a man. He is the second son of king Drupada!"

"Yes, that's who she is in this life. But she is, in reality, princess Amba reborn as a prince," said Bheeshma and told him her story, adding, "She had prayed to Lord Shiva that she might fight me on the battlefield. She could not do it as a woman, of course. So she was reborn as prince Shikhandi. But I know who she really is. I shall not fight a woman."

"How... very... strange!" cried the eldest Pandava prince.

"But true, nevertheless. If you want to defeat me always have Shikhandi around. I shall not fight her."

Amba, eager and excited, came to the battlefield along with the Pandavas. She showered Bheeshma with arrows but to her utter annoyance he never seemed to notice her existence or strike back in return. It was hardly a war so far as the two of them was concerned. Amba felt a surge of resentment as well as relief. She knew too well that Bheeshma could not be conquered unless he wished it himself.

The battle raged for several days. At last Bheeshma, feeling that he had done his duty was tired of war. He had lived long enough, more than a lifetime! Had he not renounced his right to love, power and glory with a smiling face to make his own father happy? Had he not brought up his stepbrothers, nephews and grand nephews with the best of love and care, living for them and fighting for them even at this age? What more could a *Kshatriya* do? But yes, he owed Amba some compensation for what she had suffered. Perhaps the time had come to grant it, to let her have her revenge, after all.

Bheeshma threw down his weapons when Shikhandi attacked him the next time and allowed the Pandavas to overpower him. Everyone was heartbroken at the fall of this great warrior whom death could only overtake at his own will. But a smile of satisfaction lurked about his lips as he blessed his grand nephews for the last time. In his mind's eye he could see a young and beautiful girl with flashing eyes, crying for revenge. Well, she had it now. Bheeshma had renounced the world of his own free will. Would she be satisfied at last?

A Debt Repaid

"What on earth shall we do now?"

"The well isn't particularly deep, but the ball has fallen right in!"

"So, that means the end of our game!"

The young princes of Hastinapur peered into the well, all speaking together. The black water down below reflected their faces. The ball floated across the water – just irritatingly out of reach!

"I wish I could fish it out!" said Arjuna. "It will spoil our game, if we don't."

"Do you suppose I could dive for it?" suggested Bheema.

"Don't be silly!" said Duryodhana, tossing his head contemptuously. "Who would pull you out of the well if you did? Haven't you noticed how slippery the wall of the well is?"

"It won't help matters if we quarrel," said Yudhisthira, the eldest of the princes and the acknowledged peacemaker of the family.

Suddenly there was the sound of laughter. The laughter of a grown-up man, apparently greatly amused! The young princes turned around to look. Who could possibly be laughing at them? Surely not Bheeshma, their revered grand-uncle? He never laughed at them! But this man was a stranger. A man with graying hair and a long grey beard. He was tall and erect, impressive and imposing to look at. He laughed his ringing laugh once again. "Shame on you, young princes! Shame on you!" he said, "Aren't you *Kshatriyas*? And yet unable to manage a simple feat like fishing the ball out?"

"Simple, sir?" said Arjuna looking at the stranger keenly. "You call it a simple thing to pick up that ball in the well?"

"Very simple," replied the stranger.

"Easier said than done!" remarked Duryodhana, "We'd believe you if you actually did it."

"What will you give me if I pick it up from the well?" asked the surprising stranger.

"Anything you say," said Yudhisthira promptly.

"Very well. Don't forget your promise."

"Kshatriyas never do, Sir," said Arjuna giving him a straight look.

The stranger pulled out his bow and a sheaf of arrows. The first arrow hit and stuck to the ball. The second hit and stuck to the first arrow. The third arrow stuck to the second and so it went on until there was a long stick made of arrows with the ball at its tip. The stranger pulled it up in a trice and held the ball in his hand. "There you are!" he said, tossing the ball to Yudhisthira.

The princes started at him in wonder. "Surprised?" asked the stranger laughing. "Well, this is nothing! Watch me now." He took off his ring and threw it into the well. He then took his bow and arrows and picked up his ring from the bottom of the well just as he had picked up the ball. It was really incredulous! And performed within moments!

"What would you like us to give you, sir?" asked Yudhisthira remembering his promise.

"Just this. Go to Bheeshma, you grand-uncle, and tell him what you have just seen. I shall wait here, under this tree, until he comes to me."

"Comes to you?" said Duryodhana in a disbelieving voice. "You expect our grand-uncle to come at the command of a commoner like you? You must be crazy!"

"I know he will come rushing," said the stranger with twinkling eyes.

"We shall do as you say, sir. Please wait here," said Yudhisthira in his soft voice.

Those of you who have already read the story of Bheeshma would remember that he had renounced the throne of Hastinapur and taken the vow to remain unmarried for the sake of his father. It was because his stepmother Satyavati's father had refused point blank to give her in marriage to the king unless he promised that the eldest son born to Satyavati would be the next king and not Bheeshma to whom the throne rightfully belonged. Bheeshma had gladly taken the vow for the sake of his father's happiness.

So Satyavati's son Vichitrabeerya had been crowned as king. But he had an untimely death leaving behind two sons, Pandu and Dhritarashtra, whom Bheeshma brought up. Unfortunately Dhritarashtra, the elder of the sons, was born blind and could not be the king. Pandu, the younger brother also had an untimely death. Pandu had five sons – Yudhisthira, Bheema, Arjuna, Nakula and Sahadeva. They were called the "Pandavas". Dhritarashtra had a hundred sons and were called the "Kauravas". The eldest of them was Duryodhana. Bheeshma brought them all up with equal love and care and ruled the kingdom on their behalf.

The stranger sat under the tree while the princes rushed to the palace to tell Bheeshma about the strange man. Bheeshma sprang up from his seat at soon as he heard about the incident. "Where is he? Where have you left him? Take me to him at once!" he said.

"Why, Grand-uncle, do you know who he is?" asked Arjuna in surprise.

"It must be Dronacharya, the great sage-warrior. He alone is capable of such a feat!" said Bheeshma in an excited voice, his eyes shining.

"Dronacharya!" cried the princes in awe.

"Yes, and if only I can detain him here, you fortunes are made, my boys!" said Bheeshma.

"Is he a greater warrior than Kripacharya, our teacher?" asked Arjuna in an eager voice.

"The very greatest," said Bheeshma in a firm voice, "Ever since Parasurama, who was my teacher, gave him all his own weapons, Dronacharya has been invincible!"

"And will he teach us?" cried Arjuna in an eager voice.

"I shall certainly request him. If he does, I shall have nothing more to worry about," said Bheeshma.

Dronacharaya was still sitting under the tree when Bheeshma reached him followed by the princes. The two great warriors embraced each other. Bheeshma eagerly invited him to stay in the palace and teach the young princes the art of warfare so that they might become competent warriors. Dronacharya gladly agreed and admitted that it had been his main reason for coming to Hastinapur. Everyone was happy.

Dronacharya faced his new group of pupils the next morning.

"I shall teach you to the best of my ability and with all my heart," he said looking at the eager, young faces around him. "I shall give you my very best. But once my teaching is complete and you are ready, I shall ask for something in return. It will be your *gurudakshina* – the payment due to a teacher from his pupils. Will you give it to me, boys?"

"Of course I will," said Arjuna promptly while the rest of the princes stood silent, "I shall do whatever you ask of me."

"Bravo!" said Dronacharys, embracing him. "Spoken like a true *kshatriya*! I shall not forget it, Arjuna."

Dronacharya felt from that very moment that there was something very special about Arjuna. Not only because he had spoken up as he did. But because there was an air of sincerity, dedication, and concentration about him which spoke of the true warrior. Dronacharya looked at him, knowing instinctively that he would be the one to profit most from his lessons.

His instinct turned out to be absolutely correct. Arjuna grasped everything before the others had even heard Dronacharya properly. He mastered every detail with the greatest of ease, missing nothing. He was a born warrior, naturally adept at learning. Dronacharya felt a wave of delight and satisfaction as he saw Arjuna fast acquiring all the skills he himself possessed.

Dronacharya tried several methods to test his pupils. Once he allowed himself to be attacked by a fierce alligator and cried for help. He could have easily killed it himself but he wanted to test the princes' presence of mind. While all the others looked at each other in dismay, Arjuna took out his weapons in a flash and reduced the alligator to a cut-up heap of flesh! "Bravo!" said Dronacharya embracing him, "You have done me proud and saved my life."

Another day Dronacharya decided to test their power of concentration. Placing a wooden bird on a tree far beyond, he asked the princes to aim at it. Yudhishtira, being the eldest, was the first to try. "What do you see?" asked Dronacharya.

"I see the bird, the tree, and all of you," said Yudhishtira.

"You're no good," said Dronacharya in a disgusted voice. "Stand aside and let the next one try."

Duryodhana came next, followed by Bheema and others. They too gave similar answers. No one was able to satisfy Dronacharya.

At last it was Arjuna's turn. "What do you see, Arjuna?" asked Dronacharya, looking at him keenly.

"Just the bird," replied Arjuna.

"The whole of it?" asked Drona, delighted.

"No, just the head," said Arjuna.

"Shoot," ordered Drona. The bird lay at his feet before he had finished speaking.

"You've learnt your lesson!" cried Dronacharya joyfully "You're ready now!"

"Ready for what?" asked Arjuna curiously.

"For paying the debt you all owe me – your *Guru dakshina*."

"What is it?" asked Arjuna eagerly. "It is yours for the asking, Gurudeva!"

"I'll tell you about it presently," said Dronacharya.

He locked at the eager young faces about him. Arjuna with his earnest eyes.Yudhishtira with his look of grave concern. Bheema bursting with curiously. Duryodhana trying to look indifferent. There they all were, each reacting differently to his words. But they were loyal. All of them. Dronacharya knew that. Once he spelt out what he wanted them to do, not one of them would hesitate. But the question was, were they competent enough for the task? Were they old enough and skilled enough to be able to put out the fire that burned within his heart? The fire of revenge that had been smouldering within him all these years?

Drona's eyes sought and rested on Arjuna. How young he was and yet what determination marked his brows! He is like me, thought Dronacharya. Just like I used to be, when I was his age. As he gazed at the boys around him, the years seemed to slip off, as if they had never existed. And Drona saw himself, a young lad once again, in a different time and place.

It was the time when he lived with his father, sage Bharadwaja. He remembered the quiet days spent at his hermitage and his daily visits to the palace of the King of Panchal. Every childhood memory was wrapped up with that of a dear friend who once followed him about like a shadow. Someone who was quite inseparable, dearer to him than a brother. He was none else than Prince Drupada, the prince of Panchal.

The King had noticed Drona's sharpness and brilliance and his knowledge of the scriptures. Moreover, he was the son of a great sage. He smiled upon this friendship and encouraged it. Drona and Drupada were devoted to each other. Their days of childhood were soon over and it was time for them to qualify themselves as warriors. Sage Bharadwaja wanted to send Drona to Maharshi Agnivesha. He spoke of it to the King who decided to send Drupada along with Drona. The boys were overjoyed to learn that they need not be parted and could start their new life together.

The days flew by. The two young friends, learning all they could from the great sage Agnivesha, became inimitable warriors and well versed in every scripture. By the time their lessons were complete they were no longer young lads and had already stepped into the magic realm of manhood.

"Drona," said Prince Drupada, looking at his friend, "I shall soon be the king. I want you to share it all with me, just as we have shared everything together all these years."

"It's good of you to say so," said Drona, touched by his words, "But being a king will make a difference, you know! Things can no longer remain the same"

"I don't see why anything should change!" cried Drupada. "After all, I shall remain the same man even when I am the king."

"I am happy that you feel this way," said Drona. "Who knows, I may come to you some day and remind you of your promise of sharing your kingdom with me!"

"There won't be any need to remind me," said Drupada hotly, "And I don't see why we need to be parted at all. Aren't you coming back with me?"

"One never knows," said Drona sounding mysterious.

Drupada opened his mouth to refute, saw Drona's laughing face, and burst out laughing himself. "Drona, you've been pulling my leg all this time!" he said accusingly.

"I was," said Drona. "I can't really imagine you being any different from the dear friend you have always been!"

But in spite of all their promises and intentions, Drupada and Drona's future took them different ways. Drupada went back to his kingdom where he was crowned king. Engulfed by his various kingly duties he found little time for anything else. Drona went back to his father's hermitage and lead a quiet life of scholarship and meditation. After some years he married Kripee, the twin sister of Kripacharya, a fellow sage and warrior.

Despite their quiet life, Drona and Kripee were very happy, more so when a son was born to them. Drona had never cared for wealth or bothered about acquiring any. A life of want and hardship did not worry him and Kriee never complained. She managed with what they had and did not tell her husband how difficult it was to make both ends meet-especially with a child to care for. It was not in her nature to grumble but it pained her very much to see her precious son Aswathama going without so many essential things enjoyed by other children.

Aswathama himself was too young to be aware of what he missed. He was a happy contented child, only vaguely aware that his friends possessed many things about which he knew nothing. But one day he was greatly intrigued by the sight of his friends drinking something white which appeared to be quite delicious! He realized that his mother never gave him any such drink.

"What are you drinking?" he asked his friends curiously.

"Milk!" they said.

"Milk?" asked Aswathama curiously. "What is it? What does it taste like?"

"Have you never tasted milk?" asked a friend, surprised.

"No," said Aswathama in a small voice. "At least I don't remember it."

"Sons of beggars don't drink milk," jeered a friend, "Aswathama's father is too poor to afford it." The others laughed and joined in the unkind teasing.

Aswathama went home with a heavy heart, wondering why he was so different from the others.

"Mother," he said, looking at Kripee "Mother, why don't we drink milk like the others do?"

"Milk is expensive, darling," said his mother. "We can't afford it."

The next day, Aswathama saw his friends drinking milk again. He looked on longingly, saying nothing.

"Want to drink some?" asked one of the boys. "Come, friends, let's give him some milk."

They winked at each other and gave Aswathama a glass of white liquid. Aswathhama drank it up eagerly and began to dance with joy. "I have tasted milk too!" he cried. "I've had milk!"

His friends clapped their hands and booed him mercilessly.

"Ho, beggar's son! That was only a trick," they told him. "What you drank was not milk at all!"

"It was plain rice-flour mixed with water!" said another.

"And you couldn't tell the difference!" they jeered.

Ashwathama was a little boy after all. He felt ashamed and ran home, crying. Kripee heard the story from him and her own eyes filled with tears. "Shame on me that I can't even afford to give milk to my son," she told herself. Just then Drona came in. He was surprised to find his wife and son in tears. When he heard what it was all about, his brow cleared. "Cheer up, my son. There is no need to worry about our poverty," he said, picking Aswathama up in his arms. "We shall go to King Drupada. He loves me like a brother and will find a place for me in his court."

But many years had passed since Drupada had made that promise to Drona. He was an important king now and was quite dizzy with his power and great wealth. He refused to recognize Drona! "Me, the friend of a beggar like you?" he said scornfully. "Talk sense, man!"

"But your promise, Drupada!" cried Drona puzzled and hurt. "That promise to share your kingdom with me! Have you really forgotten it?"

Drupada roared with laughter. "I can't imagine what promise you are talking of. If you are not aware of the simple fact that there can be friendship between equals only, you are a fool as well as a beggar!" he said. "The question of friendship is absurd since you are in no way my equal. The maximum I can grant you is one square meal!"

Drona had turned away without a word. "I shall not forget this, Drupada," he vowed to himself as he walked out of Drupada's court in shame and anger. That was months ago! And yet it hurt! The memory of that public humiliation scorched his soul even today. At last he was in a position to do something about it, to avenge the wrong done him years ago!

"My boys," said Drona, returning to the present, "Capture king Drupada and bring him to me..alive! That is all I ask of you!"

"Why, Gurudeva, that's nothing!" said Duryodhana with a little swaggering laugh. "I could do it single-handed! I thought you wanted us to do something really big!"

"You may try," said Drona smiling, "And no one will be more pleased than I if you succeed."

Duryodhana dashed off, calling for Karna, his great friend, and also his brothers.

Arjuna looked at Drona, bewildered.

"You never even gave me a chance to try, Gurudeva!" he said in a broken voice. "I was dying to serve you and I really wanted to pay my Gurudakshina!"

"Don't worry, my son," said Drona with a serene smile, "Drupada is a great warrior. It will need a warrior far more skilled than Duryodhana and his group to capture him!"

Sure enough, Duryodhana returned after his futile attempt, defeated and dejected. "It is your turn now," said Drona, smiling at Arjuna's eager face, "And I have no doubt that your brothers will help you to succeed. In fact, I have set my heart on it. Don't disappoint me, Arjuna!"

"I shall not fail you, Gurudeva!" cried Arjuna with confidence, "I'd die rather than return defeated."

Arjuna was naturally adept and fully trained in the tactics and strategies of war. He possessed both skill and intelligence. He thought out his plan of campaign carefully – discussing every minute detail with his brothers. As a result, Drupada, who had no fear of being defeated by a 'pack of children', soon found himself captured by Arjuna and totally at his mercy! But Arjuna had no intention of hurting him. He merely bound his hand and feet, and took him to Drona.

"Here is my Gurudakshina, Gurudeva!" he said, pointing to the captured Drupada.

Drona's face lit up with delight. Though he had every faith in Arjuna he had not expected him to return victorious quite so soon.

"Well, Drupada," he said looking at the downcast face of the king, "Your kingdom belongs to me now and your very life is at my mercy! But I am willing to forgive you because you are a friend of long standing. I loved you as a boy and I want you to remain my friend." Drupada said nothing and refused to look up or meet his eyes.

"Look up, Drupada," said Drona. "Do you remember what you told me the last time we met? You stated quite categorically that there can only be friendship between equals. So I shall retain half of your kingdom and give the other half back to you. Then we shall be equals – and friends!" Drupada finally begged his pardon but his heart seethed with anger and humiliation. He returned to his halved kingdom, determined to pay back Drona someday.

Drona embraced Arjuna. "I am pleased with you, my son. I shall make you the greatest warrior on earth. No one shall surpass you. I, Dronacharya, swear it!" Arjuna bowed low and touched his feet. Men often make such rash promises, not knowing how much it might hurt someone else some day. When Drona uttered his prophecy he only thought of Arjuna and how proud he was of him. Little did he know what the consequences of his promise would turn out to be.

The Ultimate Sacrifice

When Drona rashly promised Arjuna that he would make him the greatest warrior on earth he had no idea how much he was going to hurt another innocent and devoted youngster. This other lad was Ekalavya who had heard of the great Dronacharya, the incomparable warrior. Ekalavya dreamt of being a great warrior himself and longed to learn from Drona. When he heard that Drona had agreed to teach the art of warfare to the Pandava and Kaurava princes, he went to see him.

"What do you want?" said Drona surprised when Ekalavya bowed and touched his feet.

"I am Ekalavya, a nishada by cast. I want to be a pupil of yours."

"Well, I have no time to teach you," said Drona dismissing him, not knowing his skill or abilities. Ever since he had agreed to teach the princes of Hastinapur many of the local boys pestered him to teach them too. He thought that Ekalavya was just one of them. Not everyone could be a warrior! Drona had no time or patience for moonstruck lads who imagined themselves good enough to learn from the great warrior sage!

Ekalavya was hurt and dejected. It seemed so unfair to reject him without testing his capability. And yet.... vowed Ekalavya, Dronacharya and Dronacharya alone would be his Guru. He would not accept anyone less! Knowing full well the futility of approaching Drona a second time Ekalavya built a life-size image of Drona. To this image he offered his homage each day and practiced what he already knew by watching Drona giving lessons to the young princes from a distance. Ekalavya was a natural warrior – knowing by instinct what the others had to be taught. Constant practice soon made a perfect warrior of him.

But no one had heard of Ekalavya. No one knew what a great and skilled warrior he had become by the sheer force of will power, practice and keen observation. And also his implicit faith in the image of his Guru. Drona himself knew nothing about it. It was Arjuna who happened to see him in action one day. Ekalavya's arrows matched his own and he seemed to have better skill at his finger tips than Arjuna! His aim, thought Arjuna looking at him critically, is even better than mine. His technique is something even I cannot match!

"Who are you?" said Arjuna stepping before him.

"I am Ekalavya," said the archer.

"Your skill is wonderful!" said Arjuna . "Who is your Guru?"

"Dronacharya," said Ekalavya without hesitation.

"What! Are you speaking the truth?" cried Arjuna.

"I never lie," said Ekalavya looking straight at him, "Why should I?"

Arjuna rushed to Drona. "Gurudeva! You had promised me that I should be your best pupil and that none should surpass me!"

"So I did," said Drona.

"And yet Ekalavya is far better than I am!" cried Arjuna. "You've taught him techniques you NEVER taught me! It is unfair! Surely you ought to have given me a chance to learn the things you've taught him!

"I don't know what you are talking about!" said Drona. "Who is this Ekalavya?I don't even know him and certainly I haven't taught him anything!"

"But he told me you are his Guru!" said Arjuna. "He would never dare tell a lie about something so important."

"This is very intriguing," said Drona. "Where is this boy? I must see if he really exists or if you have merely dreamt the whole thing!"

"It was no dream. I could not dream such skill as I saw in him," said Arjuna. "He lives in the forest over there."

Drona made for the forest, wondering if Arjuna could have imagined it all. How could he have a pupil of whom he knew nothing – and such an expert one at that? Drona came upon Ekalavya when he was practicing and stopped in wonder just as Arjuna had done. But his eyes saw more than Arjuna's had. He saw the lad's concentration. His deftness. His quickness. His unerring instinct. Then he saw his own image strewn with flowers. Drona's heart ached in a manner he had not thought possible. Here was greatness! Here was a warrior – a born warrior, whom none could surpass! Arjuna, for all his lessons and skill, could never match him. And he, Drona, had vowed that Arjuna should be the BEST warrior that lived! He would be proved a liar – to himself, to Arjuna, and to the world at large! And yet.... this young lad...!

Drona's honour was at stake and he realized that he must do something about it if he didn't want the world at large to call him a liar. He stood before the surprised Ekalavya, who threw away his weapons at the sight of him and prostrated himself at his feet.

"Gurudeva!" he cried in an ecstatic voice.

"You really think me your Guru?" asked Drona in a voice that shook with emotion.

"Of course!" said Ekalavya, with folded hands.

"Would you pay me your *Gurudakshina* if I asked for it – the way the other have done?"

"My life itself is yours," said Ekalavya, "Just tell me and I shall lay it at your feet."

"I don't want your life, Ekalavya. But give me the thumb of your right hand." Drona spoke as if in a trance. Had his humanity deserted him? Had his heart turned into stone? Had pride taken over, overruling every other consideration and emotion? Whatever it was, the words were spoken!

Ekalavya looked at Drona and realized the implication of his words. Giving his thumb meant never being able to handle a weapon again! Drona was asking him to sacrifice the dream of his life – the thing he loved most of all! And yet..... how could he refuse his Guru anything on earth? Without a moment's hesitation or faltering, Ekalavya took up his sword, chopped off his thumb, and laid it at Drona's feet.

"Bless you, my son," said Drona but he could not look at Ekalavya. His heart wrung in agony as he walked away, feeling like a vile murderer. "I have wronged you, my son," he said to himself, "I have wronged you grievously in order to satisfy my own vanity!"

Drona was astonished to find his cheeks wet with tears. 'Ekalavya,' he said to himself, 'I bless that you shall be as great as Arjuna! Not a warrior like him, but you shall live forever in the hearts of men as the last word in Devotion! As long as humanity survives people will remember you and revere you as the boy who gave up his everything – his greatest ambition and asset – in order to pay his debt to his Guru!'

About the Author

Swapna Dutta

Swapna Dutta, has been writing books for children for nearly five decades with over 50 titles to her credit, including translations, published by Hachette, Orient Blackswan, Scholastic, Shristi, Children's Book Trust, National Book Trust, Pan Macmillan and others. Two of her books have been listed by White Ravens (International Youth Library, Munich) and 17 in Good Reads. Her contribution to magazines includes Children's World, Target, The Bookbird (USA), The School Magazine (Australia), and Folly (UK). She worked as Editorial Consultant with Target (Living Media), Assistant Editor with Limca Book of Records; and Deputy Editor with Encyclopaedia Britannica, India, between 1988 and 2002. Dutta has presented papers on various aspects of children's literature at national and international conferences (including IBBY) and has won several prizes and awards for her work and a National Fellowship from the Ministry of Culture.

www.ingramcontent.com/pod-product-compliance
Lightning Source LLC
LaVergne TN
LVHW041640070526
838199LV00052B/3472